Mrs Perambulator

By Mrs Scantlebury

Illustrations by Sam Ratcliffe

For G.

It was a beautiful spring morning; Mrs Perambulator felt the warmth of the sun and thought thank goodness the long cold winter months are finally over.

Mrs Perambulator lived in a quiet
corner of Farmer Jed's field, she
loved living there but sometimes
felt lonely, she liked to be busy and
feel useful.

Miss Blossom made her feel useful. One autumn day she took Mrs Perambulator down the lane closely followed by Miss Blossom's golden retriever dog, Teddy Bear and her tabby cat, Catkin.

They spent the afternoon blackberrying.
Mrs Perambulator loved being out and
about listening to the birds and enjoying
the smells of the changing seasons.

The lane led to Miss Blossom's quaint
thatched cottage with its pretty
lattice windows. They sat in her
beautiful garden enjoying the late
afternoon sunshine.

Before Miss Blossom took her home she had a cup of tea and a piece of cake, leaving Mrs Perambulator to rest and fall asleep, after all that is what perambulators do best!

It was Farmer Jed who gave Mrs Perambulator her name and said that she was very useful. Some time ago heavy snow had fallen just as the sheep were lambing. Some of the lambs got lost from their mothers.

One little one climbed up the grassy bank just by Mrs Perambulator. She slipped on the snow, and fell into the pram, and cried all night for her mother.

When Farmer Jed came to the field the next morning, with his sheepdog Joss he found the lamb and said "thank you" to Mrs Perambulator.

He said that she was "very useful" and that the lamb could have died without her help. Mrs Perambulator nearly burst with pride.

It was not always like this, once
Mrs Perambulator was loved by a
little girl called Jessica, who lived
in a big house down the lane.

Jessica loved her pram and her dolls, and spent hours playing with them. She had a matching mattress and pillow and her mother had knitted her two lovely blankets.

Jessica took Mrs Perambulator everywhere with her, in all weathers.

Mrs Perambulator did not mind, she took her to the shops, the library, the park and even to the beach!

Mrs Perambulator was bigger than most dolls prams and she could carry more of Jessica's dolls.

Mrs Perambulator had a white cotton canopy, which she loved, it had a fringe all around and kept Jessica's dolls cool while they lay in the hot sunshine.

When Jessica got tired after playing sand castles all day, her mother and father lifted her up and put her into the pram for a sleep. Mrs Perambulator's springs were strong enough to take the weight of a small child, this made Mrs Perambulator so happy.

Then one day it happened nobody noticed that Mrs Perambulator was left out in the garden overnight. Nobody noticed that she was left out in the rain. Nobody noticed that her wheels were turning brown, and nobody noticed that on a stormy night a strong gust of wind lifted her up and carried her out of the garden, pushed her along the muddy lane, blew her into a field and turned her upside down and dropped her into a clump of brambles, thistles and stinging nettles, where she stayed for a very long time.

Then one summer evening two
Girl Guides spotted her. They
got sticks and beat down the
brambles to pull her out. They
thought she would be very
useful for collecting wood for
their camp fire.

It was lovely to hear
laughter and singing from
the Girl Guides, as they
enjoyed their week of camp.

She was very sorry when they left,
but they had found her a good home,
underneath a shady oak tree where
she fitted nicely in its large roots. She
was dry and out of any draughts.

Mrs Perambulator was so busy
daydreaming she did not notice
Farmer Jed, with his sheepdog Joss,
bringing his herd of cows into the
field. She did not like the cows in the
field with her, they had muddy feet,
they gathered around her, they pushed
and shoved her and they licked her.

Mrs Perambulator felt safe living under the old oak tree with its ancient roots protecting her. Mrs Perambulator felt sure that somebody would soon need her and she would feel useful again. Meanwhile she could only do one thing, fall asleep. After all, that is what perambulator's do best!

THE END